How Do You Know?

by Deborah W. Trotter

Illustrated by Julie Downing

CLARION BOOKS

New York

Clarion Books
a Houghton Mifflin Company imprint
215 Park Avenue South, New York, NY 10003
Text copyright © 2006 by Deborah W. Trotter
Illustrations copyright © 2006 by Julie Downing

The illustrations were executed in watercolor, pastel,
and colored pencil.
The text was set in 16-point Cantoria.

www.houghtonmifflinbooks.com

Printed in Malaysia

Library of Congress Cataloging-in-Publication Data

Trotter, Deborah W.
How do you know? / by Deborah W. Trotter ; illustrated by Julie Downing.
 p. cm.
Summary: When Polly and her mother take a walk on the farm on
a foggy morning, Polly learns that things are still there even though
the fog hides them.
ISBN 0-618-46343-7
[1. Fog—Fiction. 2. Mothers and daughters—Fiction.
3. Farm life—Fiction.] I. Downing, Julie, ill. II. Title.
PZ7.T7498How 2006
[E]—dc22   2005013662

ISBN-13: 978-0-618-46343-5
ISBN-10:0-618-46343-7

TWP 10 9 8 7 6 5 4 3 2 1

To Andy, Emma, Jack, and Patrick,
my first readers
—D.W.T

To Sarah and Ellie
—J.D.

It was morning and Polly was puzzled.
Everything outside had disappeared.

"Mama!" Polly ran downstairs to find
her mother. "Where did everything go?"

"What do you mean?" asked Mama.

Polly pointed out the window. "Look.
Everything's gone!"

Mama laughed. "Everything's still there. It's just hiding in the fog."

"What's fog?" asked Polly.

"It's damp air that you can see. And when it's really thick like it is this morning, you can't see through it."

Polly peered out the window. "How do you know everything's still there?" she asked.

"I just do," said Mama.

"Can we go outside and see?" Polly asked.

"Okay," Mama said.

They put on coats and hats and mittens and opened the front door. The fog was cold and misty.

"Can we go try to find my swing?" Polly asked.

"Okay," said Mama. "Let's go."

They walked away from the house and into the fog.

Soon Polly saw the shape of the old apple tree.

"There it is," said Polly. Her swing hung from one of the tree's branches. Polly sat on it and started to pump her legs. Mama picked up some apples that had fallen on the ground and put them in her pockets.

"Look, Mama," Polly said. "Now the house is gone. You can't see it."
Mama looked back, too. "But it's still there," she said.
"How do you know?"
"I just do," answered Mama.

"Let's go try to find the pond," Polly said.

"Okay," said Mama. "Let's go."

They walked away from the apple tree and the house and into the fog. Soon Polly heard bird talk and splashing. When they came to the edge of the pond, she saw five ducklings swimming with their mother.

16

"*Quack. Qua-ack!*" said the ducks.

"Here's the pond," said Polly. "But look, Mama, now my swing is gone. You can't see it."

Mama looked back, too. "But it's still there," she said.

"How do you know?"

"I just do," answered Mama.

"Let's go find the barn," Polly said.

"Okay," said Mama. "Let's go."

They walked away from the pond and the apple tree and the house and into the fog. Soon Polly saw the shape of the big red barn.

"There's the barn," said Polly. "But look, Mama, now the pond is gone, too. You can't see it."

"We can hear the ducks."

"But we can't see them, either," said Polly.

"They're still there, and so is the pond," Mama said.

"How do you know?"

"I just do," answered Mama.

"Let's go feed the horses," said Polly.

"Okay," said Mama.

They walked out of the fog and into the barn.

Mama's pockets were bulging with the apples she had picked up. There were enough so that each horse could have one.

Polly stood in front of the first stall and held out an apple for Dustmop. He flopped his short tail and ate the fruit from her hand. Rosie nickered eagerly in the next stall. Jem trotted around in the straw waiting for his treat.

"The horses love these apples," said Polly as she and Mama moved from stall to stall.

"How do you know?" asked Mama.

"I just do!" answered Polly.

After they fed all the apples to the horses, Polly and Mama walked out of the barn. The air was warmer, and the sky was turning blue.

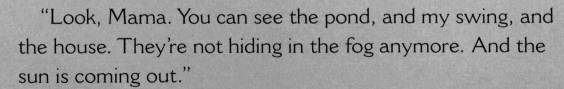

"Look, Mama. You can see the pond, and my swing, and the house. They're not hiding in the fog anymore. And the sun is coming out."

Mama smiled. "The sun was hiding, too," she said. "But it warmed up the air, and that's making the fog disappear."

That night when Mama tucked Polly into bed, she stroked Polly's hair and cheek and then gave her a kiss. As she always did.

Polly put her arms around Mama's neck. "I love you, Mama."

"I love you, too, Polly."

"I know."

"How do you know?" Mama asked.

Polly smiled and closed her eyes. "I just do."